Mariah's Maracas

By Khadijah Z. Ali-Coleman
Illustrated by Hook E. Free

To Khari,
our own little Mariah

ACKNOWLEDGMENTS
FROM AUTHOR

Special thanks to Benjamin B. Dawson, Jr. for his
never-ending patience and dedication.

Mariah could not wait to go to school today.

She was excited to learn new things, see her friends and play.

She popped out of the bed before her Mama could say, "Mariah, time to get up!"

She used the bathroom and washed her face and brushed her teeth with her favorite toothpaste.

She finished before her older brother Ricky did. He usually finished first because he was a big kid.

With fresh pigtails in her hair and a smile on her face, Mariah was soon perched happily at her kitchen table place.

"Good morning, Princess," Papa said, as he smiled at Mariah and kissed her forehead.

She nodded at her Papa and tried to grin, but her mouth was full of eggs she had just shoveled in.

"Don't eat so fast, Mariah. Why are you in such a rush?," asked her Mama, all ready to fuss.

Mariah swallowed her entire glass of orange juice in one gulp.

"I got to go," said Mariah. "So, I'm trying to hurry up!" "It's Wednesday!," she shouted once her food was all gone. "On Wednesdays we get to pick the music instrument for the school's band songs."

Her brother Ricky sat down to only say, "Who cares what instrument you get to play?"

Mariah frowned and scowled at her brother, annoyed he was always so mean.

"I'm going to pick the drum this year and be the best drummer you've ever seen."

She hopped out of her chair and stood up, making a rat-a-tat sound on the table with her spoon.

"Agggh," yelled Ricky, "you suck!" He covered his ears and pretended to swoon.

"That wasn't bad Princess," said Papa. "I bet you are going to make a great drummer. And, if you enjoy playing the drum this school year, I will sign you up for drum lessons this summer."

"Thanks, Papa," said Mariah. She looked at Ricky.

"Are you ready to leave?"

Ricky put down his toast. "Yep. Let's go," he said as he slipped into his purple coat's sleeve.

They hugged and kissed their parents good-bye and their parents wished them well. They ran all the way to get to school on time before the morning bell.

In Ms. Rio's fourth grade class, Mariah and her classmates were nervous about the instrument choices their class would have. Last year, the options were so unexciting, Mariah almost laughed.

Last year, among the choices were the recorder, the triangle and the boring sticks. Last year, there wasn't really anything Mariah wanted to pick.

"Class," Ms. Rio said, "this year, the fourth-grade instrument choices are the kalimba, shekere, maracas, drum, and the tambourine.

Ms. Rio shook two weird looking objects in her hands that Mariah had before never seen.

Penny Wilson raised her hand.

"Yes, Penny," said Ms. Rio.

"What's a ma-rah-kah?," Penny asked. I ain't never heard of that before ever in this class."

Mariah was so glad Penny had asked. She hadn't heard of it before either.

She liked how it sounded though, because it sounded like her name, only sweeter.

Ms. Rio smiled. "Well, a maraca is an instrument that is played a lot in the country I'm from.

In Brazil, children and adults not only play the maraca but also learn early how to make one.

"They are usually made of leather or a dried gourd and filled with small items like seeds or shells to make the 'shake-a-shake-a' sound." Ms. Rio shook the maraca she was holding and danced a little in front of the class, shaking the maraca up and then down.

"I want a maraca!," said Penny.

"Me too," said Craig.

Jana and Benson had said they wanted tambourines at first, but, both chose maracas instead.

Khari chose the kalimba. Three more kids in the class chose a pair of maracas, until there were only two maracas, one gold and one red. Mariah was unable to decide. This morning she had wanted a drum. But, maybe she wanted a maraca instead.

"Mariah," said Ms. Rio. "You are the only one who has not picked an instrument yet. Are you ready to choose?"

Mariah wasn't sure.

She really liked the drum.

But, she was beginning to like the maraca more.

The maraca was small enough to play and dance at the same time, unlike the drum which would be a bit heavy to hold. She especially loved that one of the maracas was in her favorite color, gold.

"Um, I think I'm going to take the last two maracas," Mariah said, "if that is ok."

Ms. Rio smiled and handed Mariah the last two maracas. "I think you made a good choice today."

Ms. Rio made a note on her sheet the instrument that each student had been given, and then asked everyone to stand up with their instrument choice.

She gave them 10 minutes to try their instrument out, and the room was filled with joyful noise.

Amber, Mariah's best friend, leaned in to Mariah and whispered in her ear.

"I thought you said you were really excited to get to pick the drum this year."

"I thought so too, but, that was before I learned about maracas," Mariah whispered in her low voice.

"I am so glad that I had the opportunity to make another choice."

After school, Mariah waited for Ricky, so they could walk home together. She shook her maraca and sang the new tune she learned, enjoying the beautiful weather.

Loving her new instruments, Mariah shook her maracas fast as she could as the school bell rang. She didn't hear Ricky walk up beside her as she shook her maracas and loudly sang.

"Uh, your voice is awful," he teased, "I have to go and get new ears." Ricky laughed at his own joke so hard, he began to cry real tears.

"Ha ha, very funny," Mariah smiled, "your bad jokes can't bring me down. I got to pick my favorite instrument and I love our musical sound."

"Wait, what is that," Ricky asked. "What happened to the drum?"

"A pair of maracas was a choice this year, so, I decided to choose one."

"Ma- ra- what? What is that thing's name you say?"

Mariah handed her brother one of the maracas and shared with him what she learned today.

"It's called a maraca. Ms. Rio said that it's an instrument that most people play in her country, Brazil."

She explained all of this to her brother as he shook the maracas, enjoying their sound and feel.

When Ricky and Mariah got home, their parents weren't home yet as they took off their coats and sat at the kitchen table to do their homework.

When their mom walked through the door, coming home from work, their excitement began to perk.

"Guess what, Mama," Mariah said. "I picked my instrument today in class." She ran to get her bookbag in the kitchen to grab her maracas real fast.

"Oh wonderful," Mama called out to her, "did you get your drum?"

"No," said Ricky, "after all that talk this morning, she picked another one."

"What did she pick," Mama asked Ricky.

"The ma-ku-ku," Ricky said.

Mama frowned her nose a little. "The makuku? Is that a real instrument or are you messing with my head? "Mama waited for an answer.

Ricky and Mariah laughed instead.

"No, Mama," said Mariah. "They are called maracas." Mariah began shaking them as she danced. Mama smiled.

"Ooo," said Mama, as she reached for one. "I remember these when I was a child."

Mama took a maraca and stood up to dance and twirl.

"I used to have a pair of these when I was a little girl. They are also called shac-shacs by those of us from Trinidad.

I had to leave my very favorite pair when I moved here to the United States, and that made me very sad."

"Really?" asked Mariah and Ricky.

They liked it when Mama told them about things she and Papa did when they were little and lived in their country called Trinidad. Mama and Papa had all types of stories that were funny, happy and some sad.

Mama taught Mariah and Ricky her childhood song "Shake Shake Shake", and they sang it so loud and long, that they didn't hear Papa come home until he joined in with their song.

"Come on let us shake, shake, shake,

Shake our maracas!

Let us shake, shake, shake in our hands!

Shake, shake, shake, shake our maracas!

Shake, shake, shake while we dance!"

The family laughed and sang together before Papa and Mama disappeared in the kitchen to prepare dinner. Mariah looked at her pair of maracas and knew she had chosen a winner.

That night, as Mariah got ready for bed, she gently laid her maracas down on her nightstand. She reflected on her wonderful day and how everything had turned out so grand.

She thought about the day and how she learned how the maracas were played in both Trinidad and Brazil.

She didn't expect how happy today's events would make her feel.

She was excited about playing her maracas in her school band and sharing the song "Shake Shake Shake" with her class.

And, with joy in her heart and a great day behind her, she fell asleep very fast.

ABOUT THE AUTHOR

Khadijah Z. Ali-Coleman is a singer, songwriter, filmmaker and poet who was born in Washington DC. She plays the djembe drum and loves mermaids and maracas. She enjoys traveling to Caribbean countries. She has visited Trinidad, the Bahamas, Barbados, Martinique, Dominica, Tortola, Guadeloupe, Jamaica and St. Thomas so far.

She and Hook E. Free live in Maryland and have two daughters named Mischay and Khari. They create books together and love to create songs together, too.

Made in the USA
Lexington, KY
29 July 2018